A NIGHT IN PURI STRANGERS STRUGGLES AND SERENDIPITY

Mrinmoy Majumder

TABLE OF CONTENTS

Preface 1

Chapter 1 We need a hotel ?..3

Chapter 2 We found a Room for Rs.150/=...............7

Chapter 3 Will he rob us ?.. 11

Chapter 4 Where is the Hotel ?...............................15

Chapter 5 We get a room at 4:30 am 19

Chapter 6 What is the Price ? 23

Chapter 7 The Pungent Smell of Burning Wood...27

Chapter 8 What an experience.................................31

PREFACE

Some journeys unfold exactly as planned, while others lead us down unexpected paths, revealing stories that linger long after the moment has passed. This is one such story:a tale of friendship, uncertainty, and the peculiar charm of an unfamiliar night in Puri.

In 2002, three engineering students from Bhubaneswar embarked on their annual visit to Puri during **Saraswati Puja**, an occasion marked by devotion, festivity, and tradition. But this year was different. Their arrival, delayed until the late hours of the night, was met with an unforeseen challenge, a city devoid of vacancies, its hotels fully booked, and its streets eerily quiet except for the distant hum of waves crashing against the shore. Fatigue settled in, frustration mounted, and a question loomed large: Where would they spend the night?

Just as uncertainty threatened to consume them, a priest emerged—a figure cloaked in mystery yet radiating an air of assurance. With no better option and a hesitant trust in his words, they followed him through dimly lit streets, their minds oscillating between hope and suspicion. The journey led them to an unlikely destination, a modest motel, where relief finally arrived—though not without its own surprises.

Through the haze of exhaustion, bargaining, and an unexpected twist in pricing, the night unraveled in ways they hadn't anticipated. What started as a struggle for shelter became a lesson in resilience, a momentary test of faith in strangers, and a reminder that travel has its own way of scripting memorable stories.

This is the account of that restless night, a recollection of discomfort, serendipity, and the strange comfort of knowing that some adventures, however unplanned, become experiences worth retelling.

CHAPTER 1

WE NEED A HOTEL ?

Puri is one of the most popular pilgrimages in India. a town in Odisha that is around 60 km from Bhubaneswar, the state capital. This incident happened while I was completing my engineering degree in Bhubaneswar. It was 2002. During that period, a couple of my friends and I made it a point to visit Puri on the day of Saraswati Puja. We followed this for the four years of our stay in BBSR during our graduation program.

That year also three of us planned to visit Puri on the day of Saraswati Puja. But was late to start the journey. We took a bus from Bhubaneswar to Puri.

Many such buses are plying to and fro for the benefit of the local people who visit Bhubaneswar to do their office work. The tickets were also very cheap and as we were all students at that time we always preferred to take such types of buses for embarking on long-distance tours. At eight o'clock in the evening, we started our journey towards Puri and reached our destination at around 11 pm.

After disembarking from the Bus, we found that there was no way one could understand that the time was 11 pm now. Everything looked normal and the common urban commotional environment was observed. So we were relieved as we all were doubtful about getting a place to stay for the night. We have not booked any hotel in advance. We had initially planned to visit Puri in the morning and return to BBSR in the night. But somehow due to some reason, we were unable to start our journey in the morning and started our tour in the late evening. That is why now we need a hotel.

We got off the bus and began to walk in the direction of the beach. There is a Dharamshala in Swargadwar which is controlled by the Bharat Sebasram Sangho. If a room is available or you are a Sangho disciple, you can stay there for a low cost.

When we reached the Dharamshala we found that all the rooms of the Dharamshala were booked. There is no room lying vacant. So we have to restart our search for a hotel room. Initially, our budget was not more than Rs.500/- but when we understood that getting a hotel room at that rate is currently impossible at the wee hours of the night, we had to increase our budget by 50%.

Nevertheless, we were unsuccessful in finding a place to spend the night. The time was one a.m. All three of us were exhausted not from our public transport journey from BBSR to Puri, but from the time and effort we expended in finding a hotel.

CHAPTER 2

WE FOUND A ROOM FOR RS.150/=

We cursed at one other for our poor preparation, which put us in a precarious scenario where we had to sleep outside. Puri is not a safe area at night, at least not during those days, as far as we know. However, we were students at the time, and we didn't have a lot of money on us. We are safe in this manner.

We finish our dinner by purchasing food items from the roadside stores that border the seashore. Eating dinner in front of the breathtaking sea waves was also an amazing experience. The sea's fluorescence effects are also visible at night. Since Puri's seawater is home to a large number of sea urchins, you can see that the sea glows when the beach's lights are out. That was a scene you should cherish forever.

All three of us were mesmerized by the beauty of this natural phenomenon. As the clock reached two in the morning, the seashore's crowd began to thin down, and by two thirty in the morning, the area was virtually deserted. At this point, the majority of the stores along the shore were closed.

Only we three were sitting on the beach and observing the sea at the quiet and vacant beach. This was a Puri we had never seen because whenever I had come to Puri, at this time, I was sleeping in a hotel room. This time, however, one of the busiest beaches in India was empty and we were still able to enjoy the view of the sea despite not having a hotel room to sleep in. I can hear the sound of the sea and nothing else. It was pin-drop silence. All that could be heard were the sounds of the waves lapping on the coast, occasionally broken by the screeching of nightbirds.

Suddenly one more sound came to my ear.

"Do you need a room ?"

A middle-aged man with a dark complexion wearing a kurta and dhoti asks us whether we need a room or not.

Although I was enjoying the scenery at the helm of the night my friends were fast asleep. But hearing his voice they also became awake and eagerly responded :

"Yes"

"But our budget is not more than 1000/="…I added.

With great joy, the gentleman who has been our savior said, "No problem, you will get the room for Rs. 150/= only."

"What"

"Why so cheap?"

"Come with me, sir. First, you see the room then you ask the question."

At that time there is no other person on the beach except we four. All three of us started to follow him without thinking much as we needed a room to stay and sleep in. Our journey and our search for a lodging had worn us out.

Every time I had traveled to Puri for the Saraswati Puja in the past, I had secured accommodations the day I arrived.

However, this time...I am not sure why there is such a rush.

"Is there any festival today?"...I asked the person who was leading us to the hotel room. But where is he? Where are my friends also? It seems that I am all alone.

CHAPTER 3

WILL HE ROB US ?

The absence of my friends and the person escorting us to a hotel room perplexed and captivated me for a brief moment. I became utterly lost in oblivion when I saw the vast expanse of empty beaches and the total darkness of the ocean. A powerful hit in the back broke through my mental block; I was surprised but quickly recovered. My friend delivered that hard punch that knocked me back to reality and gave me my confidence back. Yes, we must locate a place to stay as soon as possible.

"What are you doing here?" exclaimed my friend."Everyone was searching for you. So, what happened?

"I had lost all of you in some way. I believe that because I was moving slowly, I was unable to keep up with you guys and ended up at the back. I answered in a voice that was quivering.

"Never mind, let's move. That man is waiting in the road just outside the beach"

We were three friends traveling to Puri for a quick visit from BBSR. However, we arrived in Puri extremely late and were unable to find lodging. Just when we thought we might have to sleep on the road, a priest appeared out of nowhere and saved the day. He was taking the three of us to a motel where he knew rooms were available. Since we have nowhere else to go, we begin to follow this person even though we don't know him and have no opportunity to find out from where he has come.

"Where were you? Babu? We were all worried. At the wee hours of the night Puri is not a good place"…Seeing me with my friend that unknown person speaks with ease. But he was visibly worried.

"I just lost all of you due to my speed of walking…Sorry."…I tried to reduce his worry and replied to his query. After the brief communication, all of us start to walk towards our destiny guided by this unknown person.

The Puri Municipality's administrative authority covers 30 wards and 16.3268 square kilometers, including 3.1 miles of beachfront. Puri Beach, a naturally sandy beach, has a rich tourism history dating back to the early 1900s. Puri is located in the Mahanadi River's coastal delta, influenced by the Bhargavi River's sand hills and the shifting Bhargavi River towards Chilika Lake.

Puri's coastal beaches were formed by the filling of an unidentified stream at the base of Blue Mountain during King Narasimha II's reign., as noted by 15th-century Odia writer Saraladasa, and seconded by

Katakarajavamsa (c.1600) in his 16th Century Chronicles about this region.

The road we were walking on was the New Marine Drive Road that runs along Golden Beach. The road stretches from Light House at one end to Puri Hotel at the other.

It is also one of the busiest roads in Puri which is now completely vacant. We can't hear any noises, nor can we see the daytime hustles of this location. The partying vacationers and customers having conversations with business owners, which used to be common sights on the beach road, have all but disappeared.

The food vendors' shouting to draw customers, the battery-operated car drivers' honking, and the loud music from the many hotels lining the route are now silent. The sound of the waves and our footsteps is all that can be heard. I've never seen this location with such characteristics. It felt exactly like traversing a road through a forest.

CHAPTER 4

WHERE IS THE HOTEL ?

"Here is your Hotel"..we all stopped at a junction that is famously known as the place where "Sri.Chaitanya Mahaprabhu" took his cremation or Swargodwar after hearing this from our guide of the "night".

We all look at one another. One of my friends replied to him: "Where? We find nothing but darkness here. Only that bulb is glowing."

"Pay attention to that light. Babu. Our guide said, "Come with me. Let's go towards the bulb." We make our way over to the lightbulb. The images are becoming clearer to us as we get closer to the lightbulb. There are two stores and a very small road passes between them.

We follow the one who led us here as we make our way towards the small road. As we continued onward along the small road, a two-story hotel suddenly appeared in front of us after a short while of walking.

"This is your hotel?"..that same friend queried our guide.

"Yes Sir"….with a very peaceful voice he replied.

This building which has no sign board stating its identity is in good condition but has no light surrounding it. So it looks just like Bhoot Bangla (ghost house). We can not see any boarders; may be they are all asleep but we can not see any people also like watchmen or receptionists.

So we were a bit hesitant.

First, at this time of the night when there is no one outside, this person can lead us to his team and rob us when we go inside this building. Second, if he tries to kidnap us and ask for ransom from our parents then he or his group can easily do that as we have no third person here to help us.

So the dilemma was whether to enter or not because once we entered the building they could do anything with us and we would not be able to prevent them.

But two points are in favor of us. We don't have enough money that can benefit the gang and secondly, we don't have any options. If we disagree with the man and move away from this place we have to sleep on the road tonight.No option is sometimes better than multiple options.

"If he can't sell us to some Sheiks he cannot justify his time spent with us as robbing us will give them sleep less nights when they will see our moneybags."..One of my friends suddenly quipped at my ears as if he was hearing what I was thinking.

"Welcome"

"Welcome to our hotel ?"

A tall but slender man with a mustache and red lips due to chewing tobacco shook our hand and welcomed us to the building warmly. He instructed someone inside to switch on the lights. As soon as the lights came on, the board identifying the structure as a hotel became evident.

"The building has two floors. All the AC Double rooms are on the ground floor and AC single rooms are on the second floor. There are no non-AC rooms. Which one do you want to take and for how many days?". after speaking hurriedly the man stops for our answer.

CHAPTER 5

WE GET A ROOM AT 4:30 AM

"We want to take a double room for one day only. We will leave tomorrow in the evening.", we replied…"But what will be the cost ?"

"Sir first see the rooms then we will discuss the cost. Chotu took them to Room no.105."

"Yes, sir." A different individual emerges from somewhere. I believe he was dozing off inside. He led the way to Room No. 105. The ground-floor rooms were situated next to a small hallway. He led us to the end of the hallway and unlocked the final chamber.

One of my friends suddenly asked Chotu "Why the last room ?"

Chotu smiled and replied to him "This is the best room in our hotel."

It is a big room with one bed where three people can easily accommodated. The room also has a bathroom with modern facilities. It is spacious and a sofa and tea table is also there. This is not all. This room also has a Television with a cable connection(at that time there was no DTH or Fiber), The room was neat and clean. All three of us are extremely pleased to see the room. After the horrendous ordeal that we have to face in searching for a room, this is a sweet ending to our search. We thought that the person who brought us here was a robber or a thief but ultimately he became our saviour.

"Do you like the room ?", Chotu asked.

All three of us said in unison, "Yes."

"How much does this room cost, though?" Suddenly, I started to grow wary because there were a lot of cases in Puri when new tourists were charged outrageous rates.

Chotu said, "Come with me," and he led me back to the reception area. Although there is no room for a Reception. The ground floor verandah with a phone, table, and chair which we can refer to as Reception. Additionally, there are few chairs for guests in front of the table. I looked at my watch and saw that it was 4:30 am as I made my way to the reception.

CHAPTER 6

WHAT IS THE PRICE ?

I asked the tall, slender person we first met at the reception, "What is the price? We like the room very much. We will take it but first, tell me the rent of the room for a day."

"It's nice that you are taking the room," the person replied with a broad and honest smile. "It costs only Rs. 150 per day."

"What? What are you saying?" I shouted in astonishment. "Where other hotels are charging Rs. 500 for a smaller room than this, why and how are you charging so less?"

""'Sir, this is the off-season, and we are a new hotel. That is why we are charging a lower rate. In a few years, if all goes well, the rent may increase. But for now, we have to charge this price. I can assure you that the service will be better than the other hotels in this area. We are currently trying to promote ourselves as we are new in the hotel industry and need to establish our presence first."

"Okay, I understand. Do you require any advance payment?"

"No, sir, just fill out the register, and that's all you have to do. Pay us when you are leaving."

"OK," I replied delightfully and started to finish our formalities. But in my mind, I was thinking about the room, which is one of the best compared to all the hotels charging a minimum of Rs. 500. Then I considered the time at which they would allow us to take the room, and lastly, the price. Now he is explaining that we will receive the best service at this cost, but it feels like "adding insult to injury" in a positive sense.

After paying some money in advance, I returned to the room where my other two friends had already changed their clothes after bathing. According to them, the bathroom had a geyser that could be used for a relaxing bath after such a horrendous day.

So, I also took a bath to refresh myself. The bathroom is equipped with a geyser, a shower, and an adequate number of towels. Just like any good hotel, they provide many facilities for a nominal cost of Rs. 150 per day.

"But how ?"

CHAPTER 7

THE PUNGENT SMELL OF BURNING WOOD

I started to discuss this with my friends and was skeptical about the real objective of the hotel staff.

After having some snacks that we had purchased during our journey from Bhubaneswar to Puri, all three of us suddenly started to smell something similar to burning wood. However, we couldn't find the source of the smell. We are not burning anything in the room, and none of us smoke. Where on earth could the smell be coming from? As the sun started to rise, some light began to filter in through the window, allowing us to see outside.

Before we inquire about the view outside, we would like to call the hotel staff because the smell has become unbearable and we can't find the source of it. However, when we tried to call, no one responded. After waiting for some time, we took a bath and got dressed to visit the sea beach.

It was 7:30 am.

Upon arriving at the reception, we noticed a new staff member who appeared to be dozing off. We approached him, handed him the keys to our room, and inquired about the strange smell.

The staff member was overweight and of average height. He was clean-shaven and spoke fluent Bengali, so we conversed in our mother tongue. He informed us that the smell might be coming from the neighboring house and advised us to keep the window closed to prevent the smoke from entering our room.

We assured him that we had already closed the window before leaving the room and mentioned that we would be checking out around 2 pm, so the smoke wouldn't be much of a problem as we would mostly be outside. However, we urged him to address the smell, as it could deter future guests from staying at the hotel if it was a recurring issue.

The person replied with a nod : "I know Sir. But what to do ?. I will inform about this to the management".

"OK then,we are leaving for now"

"Sure Sir, Have a great day"

After our discussion, we all left the hotel and walked through the narrow passage with high brick walls on both sides, about 14 feet tall. We couldn't see what was happening on the other side. However, on the left side, where our room was located, we noticed a large amount of smoke billowing out, obscuring the view of the sky. We exchanged worried glances.

One of us, who is a year senior to me, expressed astonishment.: "Cooking can not release so much smoke. It is some thing else. Anyway we will look into this after coming back from the beach."

After walking for some time, we reached the main road. This time, the road was crowded with vendors and shop owners who had started their work for the day. We took a rickshaw and visited the sea beach. There, we enjoyed the sea, took a bath, played games, explored interesting objects on the beach, and drank sweet coconut water.

CHAPTER 8

WHAT AN EXPERIENCE

After spending time at the beach, we headed back to our hotel. As we approached the hotel, we noticed a gathering of people on the main road just beside our hotel. It appeared that they were carrying a dead body. Behind them, another group stood in a line, also seemingly with a deceased person. After some time, both groups entered a gate.

We became curious as the gate was located near the alley that led to our hotel. If we went through the gate, the road would lead us to a place directly in front of our room's window.

This made us realize that our hotel was located next to a crematorium, and during our entire stay, we had been inhaling the smoke from the burning bodies.

"That's why we don't smell it all the time, but in the morning, the bodies start to arrive. I don't know if you've noticed, but the smell has been lingering since we entered the hotel. It's just gotten stronger at dawn. Because of this, the hotel is empty and the accommodation rate is quite cheap."..one of my other friends whispered in our ears."

I immediately agree with him, and the thought that we had inhaled smoke from burning bodies made me upset. I was incensed not just because I could smell the smoke but also because they hadn't told us about this problem.

I advised my friends not to cause any trouble with the hotel staff, as they had at least provided us with a place to stay when we couldn't find anything last night.

"But let us all check out from the hotel and not smell that smoke anymore."

My other two friends agreed with me and we rushed to our hotel, took our belongings and came to the reception. At that time the same person was sitting there who was present in the morning.

"Sir, you are supposed to leave at 2pm? Why are you leaving now ?"

"No, we decided to go to the temple now and leave for the city."..one of my friends replied to him.

"OK Sir, as you wish"

After taking the money he provides us with a receipt.

"Thank you sir for staying in the hotel and we hope you will come back again"

"Certainly", my friend replied, collecting the receipt from the staff,we all rushed out of the hotel to the main road."

We then immediately catch a bus to Bhubaneswar. That time we give a miss to our visit to the temple.

That was one of my experiences that I had not forgotten till today.